own Tales

ERNEST ARIS

This edition ©Ward Lock Limited 1989

First published in the United States
in 1990 by Gallery Books,
an imprint of W.H. Smith Publishers, Inc.,
112 Madison Avenue, New York 10016.

Gallery Books are available for bulk purchase for sales
promotions and premium use. For details write or telephone
the Manager of Special Sales, W.H. Smith Publishers, Inc.,
112 Madison Avenue, New York, New York 10016. (212) 532-6600.

ISBN 0-8317-0970-7

Printed and bound in Hungary

THE BRAMBLEDOWN TALES

LITTLE BROWN MOUSE

GALLERY BOOKS

An Imprint of W. H. Smith Publishers Inc.
112 Madison Avenue
New York, New York 10016

Little Brown Mouse needed friends

Chapter One

ALL ALONE

Between here and somewhere else lies Brambledown, the loveliest spot in the world. Do you know it? In summer the country round about is as bright as a flag. The trees wave green leaves; orchards turn red ripe; in the river the sky is reflected brilliant blue, and in the fields the corn turns gold.

Then the farmer goes out to harvest the corn – and what a commotion he causes among the animals who live in his field! They all grab their belongings and rush away to find another home for winter.

Last summer someone stayed behind. When her family ran away, Little Brown Mouse got forgotten. How lucky she was born in friendly Brambledown. Little Brown Mouse certainly needed friends.

The harvester was coming! With a squeaking and a shrieking, the Mouse family (along with the voles and shrews and rabbits and partridges and crows) skittered away through the corn. They did not realize that Little Brown Mouse was still curled up asleep inside Corn-leaf Cottage high at the top of a stalk of corn. With a snicker-snack the harvester cut down the corn and tumbled Corn-leaf Cottage to the ground. Little Brown Mouse spilled out and rolled head-over-heels.

When she looked around, all she could see were the great big wheels rolling, and the great big blades cutting and the great big boots stamping and the tall corn falling. "Oh! What's happening? Where has everybody gone? Where's Ma? Oh! Oh! Oh! What am I going to do?"

Well what would you have done?

Corn-leaf cottage

I'll tell you what Little Brown Mouse did. She hid. And shall I tell you where she hid? Under a three-leaf clover. Now you see just how tiny Little Brown Mouse was.

Hid under a clover-leaf

The horrible harvester went roaring up and down the field, slicing down the corn, destroying the corn-leaf cottages of a hundred mouse families. Every autumn it happens, and every autumn the mice run away to their winter home.

But where is that?

Little Brown Mouse had never lived anywhere but in the cornfield. She had heard tell of the Great Journey to their winter home. But where was that?

Little Brown Mouse could not remember. Was it the hedge? Was it the road? Was it the ditch? Try as she might, Little Brown Mouse could not remember.

And anyway, she dared not creep out from under the clover leaf. The world is full of dangers: every mouse knows that from the first day she is born. Better to stay out of sight and keep very quiet and hope that nobody would notice her.

Little Brown Mouse was *very* hungry indeed. From her hiding place she could easily see the hedge where the family often went to eat their lunch. It was full of *delicious* food. There were hips – purple pods as big as Little Brown Mouse herself – full to rattling with seeds. Mmm! How good they would taste! But the ground still shook with the tramp of feet and throb of the harvester, and the air smelled of fumes. Little Brown Mouse dared not creep out from under her three-leaf clover. Better to go hungry than to risk making a dash for the purple pods.

There were hips

There were haws too, on the hawthorn – round and bright and chewy. But the air was still full of shouting voices and flying dust. Little Brown Mouse dared not creep out from under the three-leaf clover.

And haws too

There were blackberries on the bramble – full to bursting with runny black juice – enough to turn her whiskers purple!

But the sky was still full of flapping, frightened birds flying away from the dreadful harvester. And Little Brown Mouse dared not creep out from under the three-leaf clover – at least, not yet.

At last silence fell. The machine drove off. The farmer went home. The ground stopped trembling, the air stopped shouting and the dust and birds settled.

Suddenly there was a thump thump thump. Some big animal was coming – some big, leaping animal! Sharp, long teeth dipped down and *snap*! Off went the clover's three leaves, and there sat Little Brown Mouse without anywhere to hide.

"Hoppity-woppity! And who might you be?" exclaimed Hoppity Hare (although his mouth was full of clover).

"I'm Little Brown Mouse! Oh please don't eat me! Please! *Please*!"

"Eat you? Hoppity-woppity! I should think not! Hares don't eat mice! Cats and kittens and ferrets and weasels and hawks and owls do . . . Come to think of it, lots and lots of things eat mice, don't they? It can't be very nice to be a mouse . . . But hares don't eat mice. Definitely not!"

Little Brown Mouse did not want to be reminded how dangerous the world can be: "Oh me! I'll be eaten up for sure and never see my family again!"

"Don't cry," said the Hare.  "Here. Have a juicy blackberry instead. I know it's my fault: I ate up your clover-leaf and now you have nowhere to hide. That won't do. That won't do at all! I'll call a meeting, that's what I'll do. I'll call a meeting of all the animals, and together we'll decide how we can help you."

A juicy blackberry

"Not *all* the animals, please," squeaked Little Brown Mouse unhappily, remembering how *many* animals seemed to be fond of eating mice!

"Oh all right. Only the ones who don't eat mice." So Hoppity called together his friends – bugs and birds and rabbits. "Does anyone know where harvest mice spend the winter?"

But nobody knew. Little Brown Mouse sighed a sigh much bigger than she was:

"Then I suppose I'll just have to search till I find them."

"I know! We'll disguise her!"

Chapter Two

THE DISGUISE

"What a big sigh," said Barney Brown Rabbit. "Who would have thought such a small mouse could sigh such a big sigh. You're right, Hoppity. We must help her. There are so many dangers lurking out in the Big World. Why, she might be eaten up at any moment by a hawk . . ."

"... or a ferret . . ."
"... or a cat . . ."
"or a weasel . . ."

They could think of lots of animals who would want to eat up Little Brown Mouse, but they could not think how to make her safe. Then Sally Starling said, "I know! We'll disguise her! We'll dress her up to look like something nobody wants to eat. That will keep her safe."

The friends thought and thought. "It must be something very small."

"It must be something that won't look out of place in the fields."

Can you guess what disguise they thought of for Little Brown Mouse?

"I know!" said Mr Caterpillar. "Go and ask each of the flowers to give one petal. "I'll sew the petals together into a dress and we'll disguise Little Brown Mouse as a flower – the prettiest flower you ever saw!"

Mr Caterpillar
sewed it

The flowers were very kind. Violet gave a petal and Harebell gave one too. Poppy gave a big red cape and Foxglove gave a purple hat. Dog-Rose gave pink and Vetch gave white. And Mr Caterpillar sewed them all together with a pine needle. When Little Brown Mouse put it on, she looked like the prettiest flower in Brambledown.

"Thank you! Oh thank you!" cried Little Brown Mouse. "Now I shall be safe to go *anywhere*!"

"It is a good disguise," said Barney Brown. "But when danger is near, you must remember to sit very still. Flowers don't move. Do you understand?"

A bumbling bee

Little Brown Mouse nodded her head: "How lucky I am to have such good friends," she said. Lifting the skirt of her lovely dress, she trotted away to find her family.

"Buzz! Buzz!" The air was suddenly full of humming. Little Brown Mouse stood stock still – and the next moment a big bumbling bee sat down on her head. Oh, what a fright!

"Eek! Eek! *Eeeek*!" she squeaked.

"Good gracious, goodness and glory be!" exclaimed the bee. "I never sat on a squeaky flower before!" and away he flew, leaving her covered in pollen off his striped coat.

A weasely sneeze

"Phew!" thought Little Brown Mouse. "I think my disguise is a bit too good! When I was a mouse, bees never came and sat on my head. Ha ha!"

She soon stopped laughing when a great big weasel came loping through the grass. It had a fierce, ferocious face and snip-snap sharp white teeth. And there was nothing in the world it wanted so much as a little brown mouse for its tea.

Little Brown Mouse stood stock still. Only her whiskers trembled with fear. The weasel came closer and closer. He saw her! He came up to her! And he sniffed . . .

ATCHOOO!

The pollen left on her dress by the bumbling bee tickled the weasel's nose and made it sneeze: "*ATCHOOO!* Bother my hay-fever," snuffled the weasel and off he went at a trot. "And bother flowers!"

"Phew!" thought Little Brown Mouse. "If it weren't for my dress, he would have eaten me up for sure!"

Then a big, dark, flapping shadow fell over her and the sound of wings filled the air. Little Brown Mouse stood stock still. Was it a hungry hawk looking for a small brown mouse to eat? The winged creature settled right beside Little Brown Mouse – a big, beautiful butterfly who pushed her long tendrils inside the petals of the mouse's dress.

"Do you *mind*!" snapped Little Brown Mouse. "That's my dress, I mean petal . . ."

"Aaagh!" cried the butterfly "I thought you were a flower," and away it flew, all of a flutter.

Beautiful butterfly

Saved from the spider's web

Chapter Three

THE FLOWER AND THE FAIRY

Little Brown Mouse was rather brave. But she was not very clever. So when she saw a dandelion clock caught up in a spider's web, she mistook it for a fairy – a soft, white fairy – trying to get free. And as she was a kind Brown Mouse she wanted to try and help the fairy to escape.

"There there! I'll get you out! She lifted down the fluffy whiteball. "Oh Fairy! Now that I've saved you from the spider's web, will you help me find my lost family?"

Caught by the wind, the dandelion clock blew lightly away – bowling through the air as light as the breeze itself. "My Fairy is showing me the way!" cried Little Brown Mouse. "Oh thank you, Fairy! I'll follow you! Lead on!"

When the wind blew strongly, the dandelion clock tumbled through the air like a snowflake in a blizzard. Then Little Brown Mouse had to scamper along as fast as she could go. But when the wind dropped, the white, fluffy ball settled down to the ground and Little Brown Mouse was able to catch up. "How kind to wait for me," she would say politely.

Sometimes it floated so high that she lost sight of it against the white clouds. Sometimes it blew into the bramble hedge and got stuck. Little Brown Mouse did not say so, but the Fairy seemed to be rather good at getting stuck – on thistles, on briars, in trees, on puddles and under toadstools. "Perhaps it is only a very young and foolish fairy. A baby fairy," thought Little Brown Mouse and she patiently set it free. Then the wind blew and the bright, light ball rose into the air and bowled along for all the world as if it knew where it was going and was leading the way.

When the sun went down, she followed by the lights of a big harvest moon. "Go on! I'm following!" she called, although she was almost too tired to take another step.

When the sun came up again, she went on looking for the place where harvest mice go in winter. "Where is it? Can you tell me?" she called out to her blowy little fairy. But the dandelion clock said nothing at all, of course, and simply tumbled on its way across the dew-wet fields.

"Oh look out! I don't think you should go near the water!" she called. But the dandelion clock took no notice, of course, as the breeze carried it out across the water of a pond and dropped it softly on to a lily pad. "Oh! Why did you do that? I can't rescue you from there! Oh me, oh my! What *are* we going to do now?"

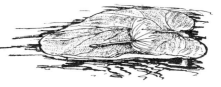

Dropped on to a lily pad

"At your service, Flower"

Chapter Four

A FADING FLOWER

Little Brown Mouse sat down by the pool and wept. "Now I'll never find my lost family! And I wish the Queen of the Fairies would come and rescue her baby fairy before it drowns!"

"I say! Never seen a crying flower before! Most unusual! Most!" exclaimed a loud, rough voice. An enormous green monster pulled itself out of the pond and came and dripped over Little Brown Mouse.

"Oh! Oh! The queen of the Fairies! I wished for you and you came!" gasped Little Brown Mouse.

"Guggle guggle guggle!" giggled the enormous green monster. "I'm not Queen of the Fairies. I'm Oggie the Frog-og. At your service, Flower."

"In that case," replied Little Brown Mouse. "I do hope you won't eat me."

"*Eat* you? Wouldn't dream of it, Flower."

"Good. In that case, I'm very sorry you fell in the pond and got so wet."

"Fell in? Guggle-guggle! Fell in! I was *born* in, Flower. I'm a frog-og." And to prove it, he dived into the water and made a huge splash.

He dived right in

"In that case, could you possibly rescue my baby Fairy from that Lily pad?" begged Little Brown Mouse.

"No prob-obbo-lem," replied the helpful frog. Maybe Oggie thought it was a fairy, too. Or perhaps he just hated to see a flower crying. He carried the dandelion clock back to her in his mouth.

Just then, one of his many many children came swimming by. "Tiny Tadpole, come and meet a talking flower," said Oggie the Frog. "They are very rare, you know."

"Not a flower at all"

Tiny Tadpole poked his small black head out of the water and stared. "That's not a flower at all," he said. "Flowers don't have tails."

Little Brown Mouse looked down at her dress. Something awful had happened. The sun had shone on her and dried the petals of her wonderful dress. They were turning brown and starting to shrivel. Her long brown tail really was showing. So Little Brown Mouse told her sad story to Oggie and Tiny, and Oggie scratched his wet green head. "Well, you can't go on pretending to be a flower, Flower. Soon you'll have to pretend to be something else instead. I know . . !

Pretend to be a leaf

"You can pretend to be a leaf – a dry old leaf blowing along in the wind. There are lots about at this time of year."

"Do I look like a leaf?" asked Little Brown Mouse doubtfully.

"You look very like a leaf," said Tiny Tadpole ". . . if you will just keep your tail tucked in."

So Little Brown Mouse wound her long brown tail round and round her waist then practised being a leaf.

She watched the fallen leaves swirling by, and she tried to drift along in just the same way. Do you think *you* could make people think you were a leaf?

Little Brown Mouse was so busy practising that she almost missed seeing when a puff of wind lifted the dandelion clock and carried it away into the distance. "Oh wait for me! Wait for me!" she cried. And off she ran, following the whirling white fluff.

"Do you think she will find her lost family?" Tiny asked his father.

"Prob-abob-aly now," said Oggie sadly. "I just hope she won't find any-bobbo-dy more dangerous."

All over Brambledown Little Brown Mouse followed on behind her 'Fairy' – up hill and down valley, along cart tracks and over ditches, through the apple orchards – as far as Brambledown Wood by sunset.

And there the silly dandelion clock blew inside a hollow tree.

Little Brown Mouse followed it inside. "I'm so glad you do go to sleep sometimes," she squeaked, and she curled up on a cosy pile of leaves while close by her Fairy glowed white in the darkness.

In the morning, Little Brown Mouse was woken by a great tossing and turning. Then a big black paw patted her down and scooped her up. Daylight showed that she had bedded down alongside a huge spiky monster already curled up inside the tree. The dandelion had blown inside and got caught on the spines of . . . Henry Hedgehog!

Little Brown Mouse squealed and started to run. Henry (who was getting ready to go to sleep for the winter) tried to catch her in his paws. "Come back, Leaf. I need plenty of leaves for my winter blanket. I don't want to sleep in a draught." The dandelion fluff came loose from his spines and went dancing away on the breeze. So, too, did Little Brown Mouse, as fast as her legs would run.

Henry Hedgehog getting ready for winter

"How very extraordinary!" said Henry Hedgehog, stepping outside his tree-bedroom. "I could swear that leaf had a long brown tail hanging down behind. And I do believe it squeaked. Oh well. Let it go. I wouldn't get much sleep with a squeaking leaf in my blanket, would I?"

And he turned back towards the warm. He was far too fat and full of food and sleepy to trouble about a leaf with a tail or a dandelion clock.

Silly Brown Mouse. Fancy thinking that Henry Hedgehog was dangerous. Silly Brown Mouse. Fancy forgetting where harvest mice spend the winter. She could remember her mother talking about it. The place began with an R. A rock? A rack? A ruck?

"I do believe it squeaked"

Chapter Six

GREEN-EYED MONSTER

Barney put her on his shoulder and carried her right up to the yard wall. She could see his long brown ears trembling with fright.

"Put me down here. I can go the rest of the way myself. Thank you, Barney."

Just then, a noise behind the wall made them almost jump out of their skins with fright:

BOWOWOWOW!

"A dog!" wailed Barney. Over the wall leaped a huge black-and-white beast. It chased Barney all the way back to his burrow. Meanwhile, Little Brown Mouse crept into the farmyard and limped towards the corn-rick. But oh dear! Who should she see watching her but a green-eyed monster – *a monstrous great big kitten*!

There were lots of dry leaves blowing about in the farmyard. At once Little Brown Mouse pretended as best she could to be a blowy brown leaf dancing on the breeze. Silly mouse! She did not realize. Next best to chasing mice, kittens love to chase dancing leaves! Keep still, Little Brown Mouse, and perhaps he won't notice you!

With a pounce and a bounce, a pat and a bat, a paw and a claw, the kitten happily jumped about amid the rustle of leaves. His paw sliced the air over Little Brown Mouse's head. His sharp little teeth snapped shut right beside her ear. Even so, Little Brown Mouse edged nearer and nearer to the corn-rick, hoping to dash inside it if, for one moment, the kitten turned its back. A stroke of luck!

Kittens chase leaves

A flurry of leaves skipped away across the yard and the kitten bounced after them. Little Brown Mouse set off to run, but her poor paw made her slow and awkward. The kitten turned back! He looked directly at her! He got ready to spring!

Just then, a gust of wind tore off one whole poppy petal from Little Brown's ragged dress. It spun into the air.

Over her head leaped the kitten. Up into the sky leaped the green-eyed monster. It pounced on the petal and not on the mouse.

Silly little kitten! But after all, it was only young.

With never a thought for her sore paw, Little Brown Mouse dashed into the corn-rick and hid among the long green leaves and the rough brown stalks. It smelled like home.

Tore off a petal

To pounce on petals

"Was that . . .? Was it . . .? Did I see . . .? Surely not?" The kitten looked once then looked again at the corn-rick. Had he really seen a long brown tail disappear inside? No! Impossible! So the kitten bounced away to pounce on more leaves and petals. It was a wonderful game.

Up through the corn-rick climbed Little Brown Mouse, calling all the while, "Ma! Ma! I've come all the way from the cornfield and I've seen a green monster and a spiny monster and a barking monster and a weasel and a bee and a butterfly and a caterpillar who turned into a moth, and I followed a fairy but I trod on a prickle, so Barney Brown had to carry me, and I've been a flower and I've been a leaf and now I want to be a harvest mouse again, all warm and safe for the winter!" It left her quite out of breath.

"Who's that? It sounds just like . . . No, it couldn't be. She was left behind, poor thing. But it does sound like . . . it does . . . it does . . . it *is*! Little Brown Mouse has found her way here! What a clever little mouse!" Then there were hugs and kisses from Mother and Father, brothers and sisters. Everybody wanted to hear her amazing adventures.

Outside the corn-rick, the kitten sat puzzling. "What funny squeaking in the top of the corn-rick. Whatever can it be?"

You won't tell him will you?

"Whatever can it be?"

The Bramb